MIDNIGHT
SWEATLODGE

WAUBGESHIG RICE

THEYTUS BOOKS

Library and Archives Canada Cataloguing in Publication

Rice, Waubgeshig
Midnight Sweatlodge / Waubgeshig Rice.

ISBN 978-1-926886-14-5

I. Title.

Cataloguing data available from Library and Archives Canada

Cover Photo:
LC-USZC4-10044 of the Edward S. Curtis Collection
Library of Congress Prints and Photographs Division
Washington, D.C. 20540 USA

Printed in Canada

MIXTE
Papier
FSC FSC® C100212

Printed on Ancient Forest Friendly 100% post-consumer fibre
paper.

THEYTUS BOOKS

www.theytus.com
Theytus Books, Green Mountain Rd., Lot 45, RR#2, Site 50, Comp. 8
Penticton, B.C., V2A 6J7, Tel.: 250-493-7181
In the USA: Theytus Books, P.O. Box 2890, Oroville, Wash., 98844

Patrimoine Canadian
canadien Heritage

Canada Council Conseil des Arts
for the Arts du Canada

BRITISH COLUMBIA
ARTS COUNCIL
Supported by the Province of British Columbia

Theytus Books acknowledges the support of the following:
We acknowledge the financial support of the Government of
Canada through the Canada Book Fund for our publishing
activities. We acknowledge the support of the Canada Council
for the Arts which last year invested $20.1 million in writing
and publishing throughout Canada. Nous remercions de son
soutien le Conseil des Arts du Canada, qui a investi 20,1
millions de dollars l'an dernier dans les lettres et l'édition
à travers le Canada. We acknowledge the support · of the
Province of British Columbia through the British Columbia
Arts Council.

MIDNIGHT
SWEATLODGE

WAUBGESHIG RICE

THEYTUS BOOKS

CONTENTS

MIDNIGHT SWEATLODGE

A glowing orange fire raged outside a humble sweatlodge. A tall, lanky young man in a heavy coat and jeans stood beside the fire holding a pitchfork and keeping a watchful eye. His much shorter cousin held the flap open to the lodge's entrance. It was midnight and glowing embers carried high through the midwinter air as the fire crackled. There were five young men and three young women, ranging in age from late teens to late twenties, standing in a line waiting to get in—towels wrapped around their shivering naked bodies. They wore boots to protect their already trembling feet from the snowy ground, a thick crust that broke through with each step to reveal a fine white powder beneath. Each held a shaker for the songs they'd sing inside. The women standing at the front of the line wore their hair down as did two of the young men. The orange glow illuminated their natural tans from beige to bronze to brown as the fire danced in their almond-shaped brown eyes. They slowly made their way towards the small dome, about four feet high and twice that in diameter. An Elder sat inside, waiting.

Each stopped by the fire for a moment to pray and give an offering of tobacco in thanks. They did this silently, the only noise coming from their boots crunching through the crust of snow. The fire again responded to the cedar thrown on after the tobacco. The tobacco burned silently, lifting the thoughts and prayers of the young people to the sky, while the cedar popped and crackled—almost giving those silent wishes a voice. Then the old man inside spoke.

"*Biindegan*, come in, my nieces and nephews. It's cold outside. It's cold in here too, but soon we'll be warm. Watch your head as you come through the door, and get down on your hands and knees once you're inside. Like when you were a baby, crawling to the outstretched arms of your mother. She's not here, but I'll take care of you. It's dark and cold and you may be afraid, but I'll take you through this.

"For many of you, this is the first time you've ever done this. But it isn't the first time you've been here. This is your mother's womb. You have come here for healing. This is a sacred place and when you leave tonight you'll feel that love once again. Come in and sit down."

One by one they took off their boots, piling them just to the left of the Eastern Doorway. The cedar on the ground tickled their bare feet and crept between their toes. They crouched, slowly descending to their hands and knees—women first. The chill of the ground pierced up through the prickly branches that lined the sweatlodge floor. It was uncomfortable and the first-timers became a little wary, not sure exactly what they were getting into. They circled the empty pit in the middle, going clockwise. The women took their traditional place on the west side of the lodge. The men sat to the east. They nestled close together with the Elder manning the left side of the door—a silhouette. The glow of the fire outside highlighted his long, scraggly hair kept in a single braid down his back. It was like an ancient, orange aura. And when he turned, the young men and women caught sight of his profile—a long, pointed nose jutting out from chubby cheeks, leading down to a round potbelly. There was a large copper pot of water to his left, with a small copper mug inside.

"*Shkaabewis*! We are ready for the Grandfathers! Bring them in."

The helper outside shoved the pitchfork deep into the scorching core of the fire. He pulled out a glowing, orange rock, nearly the size of a football. He slowly and carefully guided it into the womb of the shelter and eased it into the small pit. The Elder let out a deep, brief shout, and sprinkled a mixture of tobacco and cedar onto the glowing rock. It crackled and briefly lit up the tiny lodge as the already glistening young brown faces circled around the pit watched. The helper outside added six more glowing rocks to the pit before the Elder closed the outside flap. It was suddenly pitch black and the air inside was immediately thick and warm.

"These are the Seven Grandfathers, my nieces and nephews. They are here tonight to help us with our healing—to keep us warm and help cleanse our spirits. They have been with us for a very, very long time. They are the ones who gave us our teachings. They are the ones who gave us this sweatlodge." The Elder beat a water drum and its deep, hollow pulse rattled rib cages throughout the sweatlodge.

As the Elder continued to drum he wondered how hot he would make it inside. How much would he submerge these youth in the traditional *Midewiwin* ways? He had stories to tell and songs to sing. He didn't want to make it so hot they'd forget.

He turned to his left and dipped the copper mug into the pot of water, then scooped some out and splashed it on the hot rocks.

"The life blood of Mother Earth." The rocks lit up and scorching steam pumped out of the pit and billowed into the tarps and branches that made up the low ceiling of the sweatlodge. The glow of the stones faded and it became instantly hot and hard to breathe. Brown skin shimmered in the dark. Heartbeats vibrated through bare shoulders and thighs rubbing side by side. The Elder splashed water on the rocks four more times.

"I have brought you all here tonight because you need this. I have known each of you since you were babies, bringing new hope and joy into this community. But that hope has been gone for a long time and I know you aren't happy anymore. None of you. It's not your fault, but it's up to you to restore that hope, and the old ways. This can help.

"We sit in here tonight because we need to cleanse our spirits. We'll sing songs to the four directions and learn from each of them. This will give you a better understanding of who you are as Anishinaabe people. This place represents the womb of Mother Earth. In here you are back with your mother. The purest you have ever been. But there is a delicate balance between here, the spirit world, and the world we know outside. The world we struggle with every day.

When I pour this water on these rocks it cleanses you inside and out. But you need to help yourself too. The most important thing is that you talk about what's bothering you, the problems and struggles that haunt you. I will sing a song for the Southern Doorway and then we'll start with the person on my left and go around the circle."

The Elder beat the water drum four times and began to sing. The young man to his left prepared to tell his story.

DUST

The midsummer buzz of crickets hummed through the grass, the noise slowly elevating like a plane taking off. The sharp siren of summer echoed through the trees and even higher, because there was no wind. The sun throbbed down on us like a drum. It hadn't rained in a long time that summer. It was a heat wave.

"Are we done yet? I wanna go swimming!"

"No! A few more minutes. You can't even catch yet without closing your eyes!"

"Shut up!"

It was a dry July afternoon and every time my little brother threw the baseball back at me a cloud of dust burst from my glove as it closed around the spinning ball. And he couldn't even throw that hard.

Tall oak trees surrounded our house but the sun shone directly overhead as we stood in the driveway playing catch. The top of my head was burning, the black hair keeping the heat close to my scalp. Richard stood about eight metres away. The sweat streaming down his face clumped the dust and dirt, making smeared dark brown streaks from his forehead to his cheeks. Maybe it was time for a swim.

"Okay, we'll go swimming. But let me try a few fastballs first," I said.

"Nooooooooo!" he whined in protest, worried he wouldn't be able to catch what I threw him. I was only eight, but being three years older than my little brother was enough to put the fear of my fastball in his heart.

I took my stance. I raised my hands and cupped the ball in my glove, just as I saw Dave Stieb from the Blue Jays do on TV. "Noooooooo!" he whined again, turning his face slightly away and blinking in fear. He didn't try to escape because he knew at some point he'd have to learn how to do this. I looked back, pretending to check the runner at second and wound up. "Aaaaaaahhhh!" he screamed.

I pulled my arm back, ready to unleash what eight-year-old fury I had, but when I followed through, I kept the ball palmed in my hand and pretended to throw. He fell to the ground still screaming. I fell to the ground laughing.

Richard got up and dusted himself off. "I'm telling mom!" he said. I saw tears well up at the corners of his eyes.

"Come on, I'm sorry," I said. "We'll head down to the beach soon! Just don't tell mom. Please?"

He looked to the ground, took a deep breath through his nostrils and muttered, "Alright." He pulled the sleeve of his blue T-shirt to his forehead to wipe the sweat, but I could really tell he was wiping the tears from his eyes. His eyes shot up quickly. "But next time I'm telling mom!" We both knew what that meant—at least a spanking. He was in control now, and he knew it. But I conceded, and he respected that. A deal that didn't require any parental meddling—only fun. Such is diplomacy between brothers at that age. Before long, we were laughing and running down the trail to the water.

We grew up on a cliff over the monstrous Georgian Bay. The water was cold but it was the ultimate refuge on those hot, innocent days. We each had our own shortcut down to the beach and sometimes I'd let him win.

These were the moments we would cherish, years down the line.

We raced down to the water and found four of our cousins already there. At ten years old, Melissa was the oldest. She was always easiest to spot from far away, with her long black hair and pink floral bathing suit. Her little brother Aaron was never far behind. He's the same age as me. Back then he was a scrawny kid but always darkest during the peak of the summer sun. Eric was seven—the youngest of us "older" kids—and therefore the quietest. It didn't help that he was a little self-conscious of being chubby on a shirtless summer day. The usual crew was rounded out by his little brother Aaron who was the same age as Richard. They were inseparable when we were all around. They were hot stepping, the heat of the black sand too intense for the soles of their feet. The mid-July sun baked the sand and cooked little brown rez feet. It was enough to drive us into the water. It always started the same.

"Hot, eh?"

"Yeah."

"Race ya in?"

"See ya!"

So began our epic, three-hour swims down at the beach. We would throw Frisbees, play tag and have swimming contests. Melissa always won. She could hold her breath the longest and knew how to swim to the rock and back without stopping. And that's all that mattered those summer days—who could hold bragging rights over the other with the smallest feats.

As soon as we were exhausted from swimming we'd towel off and it was suppertime—hot dogs and hamburgers on the barbecue and corn on the cob. All our aunts, uncles and cousins were there. The adults talked and laughed and we schemed about how to collect the most blackberries. The only downside was that we had to wait half an hour before the adults would let us swim again. We'd get bored talking about blackberries and that innate cousin and sibling rivalry would creep in again as our eyes gazed out to the inviting blue water.

"You just got lucky, Melissa!"

"Shut up Aaron, I'll still beat you!"

"I bet fatty Eric could even beat you now with all those hot dogs you just ate."

"Don't make fun of him!" Arguments like this usually led her to slap Aaron in the back of the head. They were the only two who were really violent like that, probably because they were the oldest brother and sister of the whole extended family. But sometimes that slapping was contagious, and this time little Richard went off on Eric's belly. His innocent slap left a red, five-year-old handprint just to the right of his inward belly button. Even Eric had to giggle about that. Just like that, we were all friends again and it was time to run back into the water.

I bet we'd trade everything to be there again.

In the summertime the waves lapped against the beach in hypnotic rhythms. It was the pulse of our community. We were about three hundred strong on an island in the heart of the Great Lakes. Our reserve had been settled in the late 19th century when a town was established on the mainland—where our people had traditionally set up summer camp. We were pushed out onto this island—a solid rock with no real way off. We were left to hunt and fish limited resources and gather whatever sustenance a small, cragged and agriculturally barren island could provide. The old ways withered and died as the town we could see across the water prospered—a logging town that thrived from pillaging the ancient trees we respected so much.

In the wintertime the water froze over. And if it froze as the wind blew it left claws of ice tearing up at the sky. Almost like *Misshepiishu*, the water lynx that threatened our safe solitude on the beaches of the mighty bay. Those were the most desolate times. The wind howled and the sharp blizzards kept us locked in our humble homes. People drank. They fought. It was by far the ugliest season. But we found ways to keep life pure and wholesome. My little brother and I would go ice fishing. We'd play hockey with the other kids in various cleared-off inlets along the shoreline—anything to keep us occupied.

It was a community in healing, the older generation still getting used to being stuck here. They didn't talk much about the old days or the old ways. That was beaten out of them early on. But after three generations there was a bit of a spark. Our dad didn't tell us anything about being Ojibway, but, once in a while, he would lay down a little piece of ancient wisdom. He was still coming to grips with understanding it himself. His parents grew up speaking only Ojibway. He grew up speaking Ojibway and English. And we grew up speaking mostly English. That's how quickly our culture had been scrubbed from our community.

But things were gradually turning around. You could feel it. The adults slowly moved away from drinking and partying. There were tiny pockets of people who became interested in the old ways—

shunned because they were supposedly wrong. Instead, they cut their hair and traded in their moccasins for penny loafers. But some started growing their hair again. It wasn't a revolution or a renaissance, but the seeds were in the ground. It just needed to rain.

Deep into summer we were still on the driveway playing catch. Richard was getting better. He didn't need to close his eyes as much when he caught the ball. He became good enough to talk while he threw and caught.

"Big brother," he asked. "What's a sweatlodge?"

"I dunno," I replied. "I think you do that when you get cold in winter. Why?"

"Nate was talking about it at the beach the other day when we were swimming. He said it's what Indians do."

"Well … did we ever do something like that?"

"No."

"Then I don't think it's what Indians do. I think we just go to church."

"Okay."

We kept throwing the ball back and forth, like the Blue Jays. We didn't know much about the team. We just knew they did this.

The crickets started buzzing again. And it was hot—that unforgiving and unrelenting kind of hot. I wanted to go swimming again and I knew my little brother did too. But all of a sudden the phone rang. We could hear it through the open kitchen window. And it rang again. We still threw the ball back and forth, trying to ignore it.

"Hello?" our mom answered.

"No. He's not here. I haven't seen him since he went to work this morning," she continued, a nervous urgency rising in her voice. That was hard to ignore.

"Well what the hell are they doing there? Shit."

I was staring in the window now. She put her hand on her forehead and shook it, her brown bangs hanging over her fingers and the phone receiver against her left ear. She suddenly looked up and saw me out on the driveway, staring back. She went quiet, and darted into the next room. For the next half-minute I couldn't make out any of the words in her muffled voice, but it was getting louder and faster. I hadn't heard her talk like that since our grandfather died. It scared me.

Just seconds later she rushed outside. "Get in the car," she said. My brother and I shared a quick, puzzled glance, wondering what was up. "GET IN THE

CAR!" she shouted. We jumped in the little K car, the only make of car our parents could afford. It was enough to get us from Point A to Point B, from our house to the grocery store or to the liquor store so our dad could get some beer. We had no idea where we were going because of this call, though.

I got in on the left side and my brother on the right. These were our usual seats. I put my baseball glove in the middle, the white ball scarred with red stitches firmly enclosed. My brother put his down right beside mine and shot me a quick glance, fear and confusion in his eyes. I reached over my left hip to grab my seat belt and quickly pulled it across my lap to fasten it. My little brother watched closely and followed my lead. I saw his hands tremble as he fumbled with the buckle. As it clicked shut he let out a deep breath.

Our mom backed up quickly into the turnaround and tore out of the driveway. I was so scared my arms felt weak. I saw anxiety in the reflection of my mother's eyes in the rearview mirror—an expression I had never seen before.

"Mommy, what's wrong?" I asked.

No answer—just a look of sheer determination behind the wheel, intensely focused on getting us where we had to go. Richard and I looked at each other again. He was afraid, so I gave him a forced smile.

Before long we were tearing up the dusty rez roads. Small rocks kicked up and pelted the floor beneath us. Each sharp *thok* louder as mom built speed. The beige four-door economy car tore past the dark green trees that hung over the dirt road until, like emerging from a portal in the bush, we gradually encountered civilization. Past the hydro line, Grandma's house, and further. Dust kicked up and curled behind us as we left the dogs that chased us at random spots on the road. They stopped in their tracks, but continued to howl after us. I leaned up against the back seat to look and saw them pacing in circles, irritated that another one got away. Our car picked up speed again, and their barks and yelps faded quickly behind us. Mom had our newest little brother inside her and I worried she was driving too fast.

We drove by the baseball field where we didn't have the guts to show up. All the older kids played there every day in the summer but I wasn't good enough yet. I was looking forward to the day I could finally step into the batter's box with the cool older guys. But that would take time and I was preening my little brother to get there too. That's how you earned your stripes on the rez.

We drove past the church where we'd be on Sunday and we took a sharp right, Mom cranking the steering wheel hand over hand and stomping on the brakes. Up the old rail line that had been turned into a road, tearing up the dust, past the prefabricated houses that Indian Affairs had built in our community. Trucked in one half at a time, then fastened together by community labourers. All those houses looked the same but at least it was someplace kids could call home.

Richard stared down at clasped hands and wouldn't look out the window. "I'm scared, big brother" he said, a slight tremble in his voice. I couldn't fake a smile this time. He looked across the console at the back of our mother's head for some sort of reassurance. She didn't look or say anything.

Finally, we got there—the big sandpit in a secluded part of the community. We parked on the ridge overlooking trucks, cop cars, and bulldozers. If you stood high enough you could see the water on the other side of the pit. The trees stood complacently, already well aware of the tragedies that could unfold. As I got out of the car, I could feel the tension weigh us all down like a spring fog. There were cars everywhere. People were swearing and pointing. I didn't like it.

I saw some of my uncles there and some older cousins, but it was almost like I didn't know them. Their eyes were so serious. They wouldn't even acknowledge us. Their cutting gazes could mow down trees. Fingers on the trigger, ready to do it if they had to. I was afraid of them but admired them at the same time.

The dust was kicking up and hanging heavy over the whole tumultuous midsummer dance about to get underway. People walked around, more cars showed up and more of our community members brought guns.

And the tense standoff began.

The reason it all happened was because a rail line crew showed up to dig out some more sand. There used to be a CN line that ran through our community to a shipping harbour on the northwest corner of our island. It was owned and operated by the town across the water. The trains couldn't run through here anymore though, because the lines had been torn out. Still, here they were. The company sent trucks and the crew was loading them up and getting ready to ship out.

It was a peaceful protest at first. Elders and children standing in front of the machinery, blocking them from going any further. Chanting, "This is OUR land!" and holding up signs they painted that morning. That's how it should have played itself out, but things changed.

The police arrived knowing some of us had guns. We were ready to fire and keep this sand home—the sand that held us up for thousands of years. Grains of sand were all we had left. They were the only constant for generations. The sand held us up as our old way of life was brutally uprooted and left to wither. It wasn't just sand they were digging up and hauling away. It was identity, tradition, the bond between Mother Earth and her children—us. This is something I learned that day, but never realized it until much later in life.

There was a line of our community's own warriors standing in front of the machinery. Men in their twenties and thirties with bandanas over their faces, wearing sleeveless T-shirts, jeans, and work boots. Even though they tried to hide their identities I still recognized all of them—Kevin's big brother Kenny, my uncle Bob and the one with the thick glasses, red bandana and sawed-off shotgun—my dad.

For those first couple of hours it was oddly quiet. Nothing really happened. The rail crew just sat in their idle vehicles, cracking jokes and pointing. This really didn't have anything to do with them. They were just following orders. Our own guys sat in truck beds, holding their weapons and smoking cigarettes. Joking too, in typical 'Nish fashion. Under different circumstances I'm sure everyone would have kept good company over a couple of beers. Salt of the earth kind of people, just trying to do things right and keep their kids fed.

Suddenly one of the bulldozers lifted its blade. It crept up slowly, then slammed it back down to the sand. Everyone jumped out of the trucks and there was a quick succession of clicks as bullets went into chambers and as shouts came from the Indian side.

"What the fuck?!" shouted Kenny.

"Get that shit out of here!" followed Uncle Bob, Melissa and Aaron's dad.

"You better not fuck around here, asshole!" I was sure that last one was my dad.

And the barrels were raised, pointing more at the five-thousand pound machines than the people in them. The dust finally settled again, making everything eerily transparent and real.

The cops rushed down over the ridge. Some were outfitted in SWAT gear, bulletproof vests and helmets, holding automatic rifles with clips large enough to cut our whole community down. "Drop the weapons!" some shouted. They were ready for a battle and it was right here in front of them.

Some of the guys obeyed. Others were dead-set

on making a statement.

They were finally feeling proud of our community and they weren't ready to give that up. It was the traditional tie to the land that inspired them. They finally had something to stand up for and there was no way in hell they would back down. At that moment, identity came rushing back like a flood. Like white-capping waves off the bay, crashing into the mundane beaches of their spirits. Something not many of them had ever felt.

It was pure passion—a love for who they were and what they stood for.

It was my father who stood out front. From what I knew of him at that age he was usually a quiet, peaceful man. His shotgun was raised, pointing dead at the line of trucks and bulldozers in front of him. The cops kept yelling at him. They even called him by name. He went to high school with some of them. From where I stood, I could see my uncle speaking quietly behind him, trying to persuade him to lower his gun, but nothing was getting through. My father stood stoic, determined. I could see tears streaking from his eyes.

I really don't know or remember what happened next. I don't know if my dad was ready to go out in a blaze of glory or if he had a nervous twitch in his trigger finger. But he shot his gun, spraying the pellets into the blade of the bulldozer right in front of him. It was nowhere close to any of the crew, but close enough to spring the police into action. They opened fire.

I heard six sharp cracks from their pistols and rifles and six bullets tore through my father, into his lungs, his stomach, his heart. As he crumpled, one last bullet crashed through his skull. And just like that my dad was dead. My uncle ran to him as he lay on the ground, the last few pulses of his heart shooting blood out from his head and chest. His cousin Percy shot back at the cops and in a split second he was dead too. My mother, grandmother, and aunts went into hysterics. From across the pit, I looked at what used to be my father—a man who was finally coming into his own. Finally proud of who he was and ready to tell us what a sweatlodge was all about. I wanted to hug him so badly, but I knew I couldn't.

Every summer I took my youngest brother to his grave. The cemetery is at the major fork in the road of our community and there's no going anywhere without being reminded of who is buried there and why. We drove by the rows of tombstones. We sat, in silence most of the time. He never knew his dad. Neither did I, really. But my dad died in a watershed moment for our people. He died for what he had

denied and ignored for so long but wanted to embrace
with every ounce of his spirit. He never got to tell me
any of these things, but he didn't have to. On that dry,
dusty summer day all those years ago I saw it in his
eyes. The tears of a thousand generations streaming
down his masked face, ready to die for us. Not just
his sons and his wife, but for everyone who ever lived
here.

When sand turns into dust it becomes so fleeting
that we hardly pay attention. We bat it away, trying to
keep it out of our eyes. We wipe it from our clothes
and shoes. But it floats so freely, ascending to heights
we could never imagine. And then it finally settles,
back under our feet. Keeping us strong. Letting us
stand proud, grounding us in who we are and who
we'll become. It keeps our martyrs at rest, but the
dust comes up once in a while to embrace us and
keep us safe.

Another cup full of water splashed across the rocks,
creating a volcanic swoosh of steam into the tight,
thick air. "These natural elements all around us are
bound to the land—to Mother Earth—and we are at
her mercy," he said. The Elder threw the tobacco and
cedar mixture on top of the rocks. The sharp crackle
followed. The rush of steam and the quick pops of

the cedar in succession drove the point home. In the dark, the Elder turned to his left.

"Your father gave his life for our land and our people. No one will ever forget that. Not too long ago we lost our way and we still haven't found it. But he helped point us in the right direction and we'll get there again. We are here tonight to honour him and what he accomplished."

In the dark, the young storyteller wept silently. Tears and beads of sweat rolled down his cheeks. It was hard for him to recount how he saw his father killed when he was just a boy—more than twenty years ago—but he already felt better. More importantly, he was proud.

"When I was a boy my mother and father took me in the sweatlodge," continued the Elder. "They spoke to me in our old language all the time—our high language. These were the days just after our people were forced to settle here. The white man left us alone, but not for long. Some would come in uniforms with guns, like some kind of police. Others would come in long, black robes and tell us our way of life was wrong. We tried to keep the old ways going. But whenever we did a sweatlodge, the men in uniforms with guns would shoot at the lodge.

Nobody was ever hurt, but they wanted to scare us away from doing this. So we had to stop doing them during the day.

We did them at night, in the middle of the bush, so no one would see. It was the last thing we held on to from the old days. Even the Elders were too afraid to speak the language anywhere."

The water drum beat four times and the Elder broke into another song. A melody centuries older than everyone sitting in the sweatlodge combined. It was far from harmony—most of these kids had never heard these songs before. But they tried to hum along, following the strong baritones of the Elder. The next young storyteller shook her small, percussive instrument to the beat as best as she could. It sounded like little rocks in a thin wooden bowl and it eased her anxiety about sharing her story with everyone in the circle. But the song stopped, and the butterflies in her stomach returned. She cleared her throat and began to speak.

"I'm pregnant. I'm gonna have a baby in a few months. But I don't know what it's like to have a family. My parents drank and fought all the time. And my big brother, he tried but ..." Her voice broke and she began to weep. She wanted to tell her brother's story here tonight, as he would have. Never a day passed that she didn't think of him. He saved her life.

Water splashed and the steam shot up and poured on them, beads collecting on their hot brown skin. The teenaged girl felt her brother's spirit strong in the sweatlodge as she gathered herself to tell his story. It was as if he spoke to her directly and she channelled him to the others.

"The roof of our house leaked lots when it rained. My brother's room got wet the most. I know he hated that."

SOLACE

The wind blew across my cheek. Such a sensual morning kiss. It was actually a comfort, beckoning me to face an otherwise dreary existence. Why do I think like this? Where do these words come from? I could hear the raindrops falling heavily, like thousands of tears on a desolate trail into oblivion. I'm not gonna leave today, I thought. Not yet. I'll wait until it clears up—maybe later this week. I cast the tattered blankets aside and rose from the solitary mattress. The round blue bucket in the corner was full. I strategically placed it there to capture the rain I knew was coming. The house was no fortress. We are all at the whim of what She throws at us. It's both humbling and nurturing and I couldn't wait to join Her—to fit in with what she had planned.

Suddenly the bucket spilled over. The blistered yellow tiles on the floor were already peeling but I figured I may as well save what I could. I picked up the bucket and was about to take it to the bathroom to dump it in the sink, but the stiff grey of the overcast sky caught my eye. I walked over to the window, bucket in hand, to face the soft, sobering draft. I need this moment, I thought. I have to stand here. The clouds were like a gentle shield, lining the barren fields and dirt roads, laying an unfulfilling dose of rain. Why did they put us here?

I took a deep breath. I figured I had better savour these precious little doses of oxygen with that painful reminder creeping back in. I looked down at my feet—so horribly blistered and calloused. I wished I had a pair of those shoes the white kids could afford. Looking up, I realized the sun wasn't going to come out today so I turned around to go spill out the bucket of rain.

The water made a soothing swooshing sound as it spiralled down the drain. It's the little things that make me want to stay, I thought. There are pleasant delights in the most basic details of day-to-day life. But those things didn't comfort me anymore. There was that mirror and a random glance at it evoked a barrage of emotions. What is, what could have been, and what could never be—I hated that image, but I pitied it at the same time. I don't know how long I was looking in the mirror, but I realized I probably missed the school bus. I had a test that day—geography. It's kind of funny and ironic looking at maps. It's like looking in a mirror. Dreams unresolved, lives shattered and a life that was both taken away and predetermined. I flicked on the light to look around at my dank and dingy surroundings. Is that why I wanted to leave— to start somewhere else far away? Is it because I had such an overwhelming sense of self-pity? Other kids have it worse, but waking up each day for me was like a fiery dagger in the heart. Sometimes I wished there were more knives of revelation. Why do I know these words? I don't want to ask questions anymore.

At that point in my life I was used to the potent tide of despair. I wasn't looking for sympathy—it's just where my head was. I looked into my eyes—

those brown, deep-set almond-shaped eyes—for some kind of answer. But it would never come because it was there all along, with an excruciating reminder every single day.

My skin is brown, I thought, looking in the mirror, and that's never going to change. I hated my brown skin. I hated what I saw in the mirror. If I was anything, I could be a model—maybe a movie star. At least a famous writer like those that we talk about in English class. Maybe that's what my test was supposed to be in. I took the matted brush and started straightening my long, black greasy hair. I shook off the regular cloak of self-pity and tried to get to school in time.

I remember walking to the end of the driveway and waiting for the bus that day. I kind of wished it wouldn't pick me up—that it had broken down or something. But I also wished it was some kind of magical caravan to parts unknown—to a wild paradise thousands of miles away from here. Somewhere that would accept me for who I was and let me fade away on my own terms. That's what really mattered to me then, my own terms. I was sick of the whole facade—pretending to be happy, pretending not to care. Kev and Tommy didn't care. At least they said they didn't. "I hope they're not on the bus," I thought, because I really didn't feel like skipping school today and getting drunk and high over at the beach. That routine got lame after a while but it was all I really had to look forward to.

But sure enough, the wagon was there right on time. I was the first one on the route, so as I did everyday I said "Hi" to Deb the bus driver and took my seat at the back. It was those moments I really savoured—the lone traveller on a bus. Some days I wished she would take the highway instead of the road to town. Deb, with her permed hair, and me, on some fantastic voyage to a realm of unlimited possibilities. A place of new scenery and opportunities—a chance to not be me and to realize these dreams of conquest and success. Doing who knows what, just something new.

But it didn't happen that day. Tom was the next to be picked up. There he was, waiting impatiently for the bus to grind to a temporary halt and let his sorry ass in. He stood there, red football jersey and baggy jeans with a backpack full of most likely everything imaginable, other than schoolbooks. He was smiling, as always. I don't know how he did it but he always managed to be pretty upbeat. He hopped on and scurried to the back to take the hard, pleather seat next to me.

"S'up bro?" he asked. "Fuckin' Mondays, eh? Well I don't really feel like the normal Monday bullshit so what you say we just bail?"

"I dunno man," I replied. "I have some bullshit test today, but I really shouldn't blow it off."

"Maybe this will change your mind. My old man passed out on the shitter this morning, so I lifted it from his room. Check it out!"

He pulled a 26er of rye out of his bag and caressed it up and down, a devious grin on his face. My mouth watered. There was something about booze I couldn't resist.

"Looks good," I said. "But if I miss another day, Mr. Adamson is gonna expel my ass."

He shook his head, grinning. "You're such a browner. What the fuck you still doing around here anyway?"

I didn't know. I shrugged, trying to deflect the question and turned to look out the window. The clouds were breaking off in the distance, over the trees. And I realized this was a dead-end routine that wasn't gonna get me anywhere. But I stayed quiet.

"When Kev gets on you'll change your mind," he said.

And the bus carried on. Picking up kids with wild-eyed ambitions but slowly shattering dreams. That's what rez life will do to you. If you had some kind of glimmer of hope, it would be cut down eventually. Luckily this was only the high school bus. All the younger kids went to school on the reserve so they were on another bus. Unlike the inconsistent handful of high school students, the younger kids were all still in school so their bus was full. Many of us had already dropped out. So, luckily the younger ones didn't have to see what unfolds when you're a redskin, pissing away opportunities that weren't already smashed.

Deb stopped in front of Kev's. He stepped up onto the bus, his black ball cap turned backwards and shades pressed tight to his face. He was smoking a joint just before the bus showed up because we could already smell pot on him. So sure enough, he had a big bag of it. It was decided we were gonna cut out of school. But just for the morning. I really had to get that test done.

Another wasted day and I was back for another unpredictable evening at home, slowly sobering up and coming down.

Kev and Tom twisted my rubber arm into skipping and getting drunk and high. But it doesn't really matter, I thought. Mom's drunk. So's Dad. He's passed out, but I'm sure he didn't go down without a fight. That is, without beating the living shit out of her. I always wished I was there for that. Not to protect her—she can be really dumb sometimes. But for Jacob and Kendra. I wondered if they did the same thing I did at that age when our waste-case parents got drunk and beat the shit out of each other. When I was six—the same age as Jacob—I remember I used to get a little nervous every time I saw one of them come home with a case of beer. By that age I already knew what the clank of those twenty-four brown bottles meant—nothing but a nightmare for an innocent child. A slight chill would work its way up my spine but I would try to ignore it. Ignore the impending melee, the fixed chaos that is domestic life on the rez.

It would always start out the same. Everything was happy. Mom would make supper, we'd sit around and they'd gradually make their way through the beer at the wobbly, duct-tape-secured table. It was in those fleeting, artificial and forced moments that I actually felt loved. They both seemed so happy, taking turns with me on their knee, telling me how good a kid I was. Not long ago I realized why I thought all the happiness in my life wasn't real—it was borne out of these false, impaired moments. We pretended we were something we were not, all because we could. The booze helped us do that. Not me, at that point, of course. At six, I still had hope. Still hoped for the happy and serene life I saw all the white kids enjoy on TV. Hoped for that degree of "normalcy," whatever that was.

Then it would turn.

"All you fucking do is drink!"

"All you fucking do is bitch at me! Fuck off!"

"What kind of example are you setting for your son? You haven't had no job in three years!"

"At least I show him how to be a man! Not no pussy!"

"How? By beating the shit out of your wife? I carried him inside me!"

My dad would lower his chin slightly and his brown eyes would cut straight at her, accentuated and intensified by his thick, bushy brows. It was a glare that could freeze a heart. His breathing got deeper and louder, and so did hers, in defence. She knew what was coming.

And then it would start. By that point I was pretty good at predicting the routine. All it took was a misplaced word, a misdirected stare. They sat at opposite ends of the table, waiting for the other to make the first move. There was a tense, thick hatred in the air between them, borne of the same passion that brought them together to create this family. Without warning, my dad swept his arm across the table, knocking five or six empty bottles to the floor in a wild crash. He stood up quickly and kicked his chair out behind him.

As soon as I saw that, I was gone. I would run to my room, plug my ears, and lie in my bed. I would keep my ears plugged until they were long passed out. In the morning, I would get up with the sun and get dressed for school. Walking to the bus was easy, but explaining to the teacher why I didn't have breakfast or a packed lunch was not.

And ten years later nothing has changed. Sure, there were attempts at sobering up on both sides. Things had changed when sister Kendra was born. I was eight and was absolutely elated at having a younger sister, someone else to help carry me through this. And Mom and Dad made changes as well. That was the longest I'd ever seen them sober and I think that's when I got my first dose of what some people call happy.

There was a relapse but a year after mom found out she was carrying again. Jacob came soon after. The temporary solace returned only to be ripped away again by the innate dysfunction that was our version of contemporary Aboriginal family life.

So here we are, once again on the downward red spiral. I don't know why I always worried so much about that. Sometimes I just wanted to get drunk and high every day like the boys did. I tucked my siblings in and went to bed.

Kendra and Jacob were the only reason I wanted to stay. But what kind of example would I set? I really wanted to be strong—to show them that this kind of life wasn't that big a deal, and as long as you can get through it, you can be a better person. And maybe we can reverse the horrid cycles that will continue to reverberate through the generations if nothing is done. All you have to do is take hold, be the example, give the middle finger to all the external forces that keep driving you and your people down. Booze. Dope. Asshole teachers. The rich white kids at school that stick their noses up at you, already convicting you of being a drunk, quitter, lowlife, scumbag Indian. The only thing I wanted to make sure Kendra and Jacob understood was that they didn't have to spend their lives dealing with all that shit if they didn't want to.

So there I was, walking those loud and affluent halls once again. I guess every once in a while you have to face the music and actually go to class. You can't say "fuck it" to everyone and everything all the time. The condescending glares and snide comments bounced off of me. Yeah, jerk, I'm in the same class as you. Yeah, I'm an Indian. Yeah, I'm smarter than you. But to you, I will always be a savage, not a counterpart.

I took my seat in the back corner. Mr. Simon scoured the room, taking attendance. He paused and gave me a brief, cutting glare. I didn't see it though—didn't feel it. I didn't want to because I knew. I was going into yesterday's test with a strong A. I found Grade Twelve English easy—some would say too easy.

The class went on with a mundane discussion about some 20th century author who wrote about things I really didn't care about. Leaving a private school to go on a soul-searching journey—a wild adventure across the country that would define an entire generation. *Catcher in the Rye*. Yeah, right. I pretended to listen as I stared blankly into the void just a metre in front of my face. It was the only space that belonged to me and it was breached too often.

The period-ending bell rang. I snapped to, quickly packed my book and tried to rush out of the room. But I was called back. "Where were you yesterday?" asked my teacher.

"Sick," I nonchalantly replied, hoping to get this tired routine over with as soon as possible.

"That's bullshit. You don't have a note and there were no calls into the office. You knew how huge that test was."

"Yeah, maybe. Whatever."

"Whatever?!"

I shrugged. Mr. Simon turned a hard shade of red and a vein emerged from his forehead, starting just above the centre of his brow and following a forty-five degree angle up to his thinning grey hairline.

"You are easily the most talented student in the class. Why are you wasting it?"

"I dunno. I don't really need it and I don't give a shit."

"Please," he begged. "David … " He said my name, which stung like an infant bee on a small corner of my heart. My parents hardly ever called me by name, so it reverberated through the empty classroom. "Don't throw this away. I want to help you. You have to understand what you have and what you can do with it!"

I didn't feel like arguing, so I agreed to meet him next week after class and go over some options for my future—my beyond high school future. I really didn't have any plans for that anyway, so I said yes to humour him and shut him up. "I'm tired of these people telling me what's best for me," I thought. "Only I know that. I know exactly what it is and it isn't in any stupid book." I went home, did the pseudo-family routine and patiently awaited sleep. That's where I could really be what I wanted.

Every night I lived a new life, somewhere far, far away, a place where life was real and happy—a place without pain. Maybe in a city somewhere, or a bigger town, so my dad could work. We'd probably live in a small house like this, but at least it would be nice. I'd be getting ready to finish high school, being a good role model for my little sister and brother. We'd have a routine that kept us all busy and happy. Jacob would just be starting hockey and maybe Kendra would be playing the flute in the school band. But these were all just dreams. Our parents were both high school dropouts and never really worked. What kind of jobs would they get in another place? After every new lifetime came the crushing disappointment of waking up the next morning and returning to mine.

A few more days went by. Mom and Dad were on pretty good behaviour. I think maybe Auntie Edie threatened to call Children's Aid on them not long ago so they were giving sober second thought to staying clean. The way gossip runs through the rez, any news of someone's kids being taken away would spread faster than summer wildfire. Although I knew they were trying to save face in this faceless community, I liked to think they were actually behaving because they loved us and didn't want to lose us. Well, Jacob and Kendra anyway. There was still some shred of hope for them. You could still see a flicker of faith and love in their young eyes. They had already seen so much so soon, but it takes a lot more rain than that to douse the innocence and compassion in the soul of a young child. It tore me up so much sometimes I couldn't look them in their beautiful round, brown faces with their glowing almond-shaped eyes, already a little worn from shedding so many tears.

I skipped school that day for the regular reasons (life sucks, I'm too talented for my own good, I don't know who I am, I'm too self aware, my parents are drunks, poor me, blah blah blah) but I didn't feel like getting drunk or high. I just wandered around. Took the usual bus to town for school, but instead of walking through the doors I made a left and headed down the street to the river. Just felt like chilling there for the morning. I wanted to take a good look at these things. I took a seat, lit a smoke and looked at the budding leaves on the branches jutting out over the water. Pollen floated high overhead. The perennial scents of spring crept through the air—life coming into bloom. This is the only time of year when people notice what's alive, what is growing, maturing—what is distinguishing itself from all other entities around it. And if this thing, whatever it may be, is nourished, it can move the earth. If it gets enough rain, the smallest tree can grow to shelter a struggling family through the toughest times.

But spring never lasts and neither does the attention. Screeching tires on the adjacent street brought me back to Earth and wiped many of the refreshing riverside smells away.

The older you get on the rez, the less people care about how you turn out. That was me, I guess. I was doing special things. It said so on the piece of paper the school sent home with me every few months but I had no idea because no one else seemed to care. I know Kendra, Jacob and some of our cousins looked up to me because I was older than them. Going to school in town, an almost entirely different world, impressed and appealed to them, I suppose. On the other hand, I'm pretty sure I intimidated my parents because of those small victories in the classroom.

I walked from town back to the rez, which took about an hour. It's almost a rite of passage during your teenage years. You go to parties in town and stumble back home in the middle of the night. It wasn't always a stumble, though. Sometimes you couldn't find a ride in the middle of the day, after baseball, hockey or just hanging out.

Back on Indian Land I revisited my favourite childhood haunts. I hadn't told anyone I was leaving, so going to places like the Pines where we used to camp was bittersweet. So was going to Chuck's Rock where we'd daringly jump into the lake in the heat of summer, and to the inlet by Kev's grandma's where we played hockey in the winter. Happy, colourful memories lapped into my head like summer waves, each more intense and pronounced with every site visited.

Then there were other places like the beach or the Eagles' abandoned barn where less innocent memories fluttered about. As we got older, these were some of the places we came to catch a buzz. I had my first shot of whiskey on that rock over there. I smoked my first joint up in that loft there. I kissed a girl, Maya, for the first time behind that tree. "I love you," she said. Of course I didn't believe her, given our common loveless backgrounds. We eventually had sex there. But sometimes I wished I had grabbed hold of that love. It was also in these places, usually in a haze, that I realized I couldn't live here anymore.

Before I knew it, the sun was setting and mosquitoes were buzzing in my ears. They were early this year, I remember thinking. I figured I should probably head home. The loneliness seemed to make their buzzing echo louder but I stood and listened for a moment longer. And I remember sobbing.

"Get your fucking hands off her!" I screamed.

The blood rushed to my face and it felt really hot. "What are you gonna do, big man?" my father mocked, holding my mother in a headlock. She wasn't saying anything, but she was still conscious, her hands digging firmly into the lethal hold he had around her neck. It's okay, I thought to myself, her arms haven't gone limp. She was bleeding a lot but she was holding on.

Jacob and Kendra had locked themselves in their room. I didn't have a chance to check on them but I could hear them crying. I'd been in the door for five seconds. I burst in after hearing the screams and smashing bottles from down the driveway. There was blood on the kitchen floor, across the counter, and shards of brown glass peppered everywhere. "You fuckin' pussy!" my dad slurred. Christ, he could barely see or stand straight. The only reason he had such a grip on her was because she was just as wasted.

He egged me on. "You ain't got shit on me. You can't be my boy! This whore was fuckin' around the whole time, I know it!" He tightened his hold and she yelped. I wanted to tell her I'd help her, I'd save her, but she was just as long gone, in so many pathetic ways.

"Shut up!" He grunted, shifting his gaze towards the ruffled mane of black hair he was so close to killing. I saw my chance. I had been eyeing up a half-full forty of whiskey on the table. That must have been the spark plug, I thought. I lunged forward, grabbed it with my right hand and in the same movement, brought it quickly down against his numb skull. They both fell to the floor, unconscious.

I had to do something. I ran out to the shed and grabbed the 12-gauge shotgun and some shells. I turned quickly back to the house and stormed up to the front door. It was still open. My parents lay motionless on the kitchen floor. I closed my eyes, took a deep breath, and went in. I stepped over their crumpled masses and made my way to my room.

It was a very still morning. Warm, but dry. I knew the sun was shining before I opened my eyes. It penetrated the naked, gaping window and beat heavily upon on my face. I remember hearing birds outside calling out to one another, communicating, feeling. There was also the soft whir of a lawnmower floating outside and the sharp odour of freshly cut grass crept into my nostrils. I was wide awake, but I kept my eyes shut, savouring this sensory overload. And I remember smiling.

Eventually I got up. It was, after all, Tuesday. Time for the old routine. I tried to ignore the nightmare that was the night before, but its remnants were scattered about our desolate house. Broken glass, blood, the echoes of screams and sirens. But I smiled through it all, not really caring whether these things remained or whether the traces of abuse would one day disappear. There was hope, I guess, but I wasn't patient enough at the time.

I looked in the mirror again at that unmistakable face of ruin and confusion. I stared long and hard this time, sensing overwhelming closure and a bit of relief. I didn't hate it anymore. I loved it for what it was, and what it had been. Nobody would look at me the way my high school peers did anymore. They would appreciate me, and understand me solely for who I was, and what I was to become. The deep-set, almond-shaped brown eyes closed. Moments later I left the house.

"I'm kicking the bus's ass today," I thought when I got outside. I had my bag in hand, already packed from last night. It hung heavily off my shoulder as I walked down the driveway. Since I had some time to kill, I took a little detour into the bush on the left. "No one's up yet anyway," I thought. "Everyone around here is still hung over from the weekend. They won't see me."

I stumbled through thick brush, maneuvering past tall maple trees. They still had holes from being tapped back at the start of spring. It was a bad year for syrup because the sap didn't run well. It wasn't warm enough for the bugs but they'd be out in the afternoon, biting away. They'd have a feast later, that's for damn sure.

"Thank God the dogs didn't follow me out here," I thought. I really needed to be alone. I crept along for another fifteen minutes, burrs latching to my tattered jeans, my feet soaked from stomping through puddles, not that I really noticed. I finally came to a little clearing on the opposite side of a small mound, a nice place to hide for a few. I found a nice, grey, cold flat rock to sit on and decided that was it. I took a deep breath, looked around, and lit up a smoke.

They say tobacco is a gift, but I never really knew why. I remember my Grandma trying to teach me when I was a little boy, but my dad yelled at her when he overheard. They don't teach that kind of thing in school either. "I guess I'll never really know," I thought. Not here, anyway.

I savoured the last drag of the smoke and flicked it to my right without looking. I rummaged through my bag. There was that stupid book—*Catcher in the Rye*. I kind of wished I left it behind because it was a sobering reminder. But I quickly shook it off and got down to the task at hand.

I made sure I had the shells. And there was the

shotgun, protruding through the top of my bag. "Shit, I really hope no one saw me," I thought. "I really don't want to be found." I opened the base of the barrel and looked through. I put the red shell in and locked it. I remember warm tears streaming down my brown cheeks, but I don't remember crying.

I looked up at the trees above. They sheltered me here. The trees that defined this community and housed the ancestors I never knew, nor would ever understand. The sky was blue but I wanted clouds. Blue skies made it too hard. But if this was my solace, so be it. I lifted the barrel and pressed it firmly under my chin.

The heat was becoming unbearable. In the darkness, their eyes began creating images for them. Dancing colours—bright red, green and blue swirling a few centimetres in front of their eyes, then spiralling down a tunnel to a whole different world. The willow branches were illuminated in the pitch black. They vibrated and expanded out into the winter night, then vibrated back in like the interlocking arms of a round dance.

Unlike the young people, the Elder sitting in the

Eastern Doorway was no stranger to the sweatlodge. And he knew the stories the kids here were telling the sweatlodge—stories about abuse, despair, and loss. He lived through it when he was their age, but left. He went to the city to start a new life, very detached from his home community. He returned years later a broken man, a victim of his own self-inflicted abuse.

Sweat dripped into his eyes like rain over a flooded eavestrough. Half the people sitting in the sweatlodge had a chance to tell their stories, sing songs and pray. The Elder wiped his brow and took a deep breath. He waited for the young man sitting across from him in the dark to tell his story. He was in his late twenties with long black hair that was now matted with sweat. As the Elder's nephew, he'd gained enough respect in the lodge over the years to sit in the Western Doorway—the gate to the Spirit World—the path that represents the future. But it was a long journey getting there.

The young man in the Western Doorway began to speak. "My young brothers and sisters, I have seen what many of you have seen. I have seen the terrible things that can take hold of the ones we love the most. That happened to me too. I lost my way." He paused— long enough to let the simple by powerful message sink in with his peers, but also long enough to let the memories of his own mistakes and demise bubble to the surface. Long enough to feel it again, almost fresh. The orange glow in the rocks faded slightly, but the heat was as intense as ever. Some of the young people repositioned themselves to get comfortable in the heat. The bows rustled under them.

"When I was your age, I ran away from what I was afraid of, to try to ignore it, only to find it in another place far away," he continued. "I lived a very good life there in the city, but I lost love and respect as drugs and alcohol took over. I lost everything."

He wasn't going to tell them the details. He wanted to give them some hope. The glowing branches closed in again and cedar popped loudly on the rocks.

BLOODLINES

It was already well past midnight by the time they stepped out of the low-rise onto the avenue. Crisp, brown leaves were strewn about the cold, concrete sidewalk, scattering further with every wisp of wind. He looked up and saw the clear November night had let a few stars shine through to the city. He grabbed her hand, which was trembling and already cold to the touch. "Here, take these," he said, offering her his gloves. She left hers in the cab on the way over.

"Thanks," she replied in a soft, elevated murmur that floated above the fall breeze. She kissed him on the cheek, sending a slight tingle down his spine. His tenderness and compassion made her chest feel like it was gently twisting, sending slight tremors to her limbs. She never knew that was possible until she met him. But now, these were the moments she lived for.

"So did you have a good time?" she asked.

"Yeah, of course," he replied. "Lynda's friends are really cool." He was lying a little. He had been nervous at first—he always was in affluent surroundings. But after some wine and beer, the social boundaries fell and everyone fit in. Even after years in the city, he still wasn't used to that kind of party. They were the opposite where he came from. "Yeah, it was nice."

She gave her own analysis of the evening. How Lynda's boyfriend seemed uncomfortable most of the night due to the fact that he was moving out at the end of the month and no one else knew. How the food was already a little cold by the time they got there. He looked at her, listening attentively. Most trivial conversations would bore people, but he liked to hear her talk. He loved her. It was a love built on five years of learning, conflict, understanding and passion. A love that could now withstand most of the usual challenges and obstacles couples are forced to deal with. They spotted a cab, flagged it down and headed home.

Minutes later he unlocked the door to their building. He let her in first and it was up the stairs and down the hall to 2C. In another door and the keys were thrown in a basket. Lights went on, shoes and jackets off—a typical twenty-something urban Saturday night. She went to the bathroom and he went to the fridge to grab a couple of beers. Then it was off to the quaint living room for a bit of music to unwind.

She came in wearing her pajamas and lit up a smoke. He opened her beer and handed it to her. She took a sip and rested her blond head on his right shoulder. They sat in comfortable silence for a few minutes, staring straight ahead at the illuminated, display of the stereo. This was routine, but it was good. They were happy.

"I love you," she sighed, as she nestled her sharply pointed nose into his arm.

"Love you too," he replied. And that's all they had to say for the moment.

They did get to talking but whenever they were drunk the topic always boomeranged back to why they were together. "Look at us," she said. "All this time later."

"I know," he replied. "Crazy eh? I can't believe you were actually interested in me."

They liked to recap how their unconventional romance happened. He first noticed her at a downtown bar. "I thought you were really hot, but I also thought you were a real snob," he said. She was sitting there gossiping with friends. In a city that big, they both lived in the same neighbourhood and would cross paths randomly—at a coffee shop, the grocery store, running on the path through the park. They would share awkward glances whenever that happened. She was intrigued by his exotic mystique from the get-go, even though she would never dream of showing it. That harmonious duel played out for weeks. Then, an elderly lady fell while crossing the street one day. They both rushed to help and stayed with her until an ambulance arrived. They were forced to talk and he finally had the balls to ask her out.

Years later, here they were, sharing a home. Getting careers underway. Living the contemporary urban dream. He put his finger under her chin and lifted. He looked her in the eyes and without saying anything, kissed her. Moments later, he picked her up and carried her down the hall to their bedroom. And before long, they were making love.

He loved the way his brown hands looked, running across her smooth, ivory body. Brown and yellow hair, meshing into one—lips locking, breathing heavily, pushing hard but affectionately into each other. He lay there and rubbed both hands up her torso, watching her feel their once forbidden unity. They could both see it even in the dark. It was like a cloud disrupting sunbeams across a barren beach, an astounding marvel of nature to them, one that has been repeated billions of times.

Gasps of pleasure escaped their lips, calling and responding from deep inside one another. Like a wolf calling its mate in the night through the forested hills. The warm blanket of the moon lit the way for them to come together. Their essences reached out to dance and caress. Sharp beams of colour intertwined in sync with the tones of their passion, love and devotion. These were unearthly shades, because what they shared transcended the colours of their skin. It built to that shimmering, tremulous threshold of release. They hovered, locked together there, succumbing to the physical power of those brief seconds that seemed like an epic, sacred ceremony. They fell heavily to the bed, as if they had come through the ceiling of their humble apartment building on that quiet city street.

It was like every other time, but it was a routine they were both comfortable with. She didn't want to change anything and he didn't want to think about anything else. This was where his troubles seemed to disappear, to stay hidden under the consoling cloak of midnight. Since it was the weekend, there was no need to fall asleep right away, in spite of their physical contentment. So they lay there and talked.

"I was thinking about something you said earlier," she said, rolling over from the safe refuge of his chest.

"What was that?"

"Well, you brought something up about drawing our own bloodlines. Where we wanted our own legacies to lie. About making life and being able to control how that life turns out."

He thought for a second. Could this have been another one of his drunken tirades, one more thing to have liberal white people hang off his every word? Most people he hung out with in the city had never even talked to an "Aboriginal" person before. It was still a novelty to most of them, to have one in their presence. To have one in their home to (somewhat) transcend their own preconceived notions. Those notions passed on to them by their parents, their peers, the media, and the rest of society. He loved the way they looked at him when he waxed philosophical. It made him feel sexy and powerful.

"Yeah ... right," he said, sort of remembering. "What'd you think about that?"

"Well, I was just thinking that it was really brave of you to come out and say that. Because I know your family has these expectations of you and who you're with and what colour your babies will be," she chuckled, trying to crack a joke, but at the same time trying to slide an important point through the cracks.

He laughed too, masking some nerves. When he was drunk, he said these things to amuse and comfort her, but he wasn't really telling the truth. He was telling her the things he knew she wanted to hear.

They say racism only comes with power, but no one is above looking past colour. Most Indians only want Indians to be with Indians. That's especially what parents, aunts, uncles, and grandparents want. That's what he felt, anyway. She felt it too, but he always reassured her. Especially tonight, in front of all her friends from wealthy neighbourhoods in far away places who converged in this urban stew of colour and culture.

What he was trying to say to her was, "I don't care about that shit, baby. We are meant for each other and we are going to live happily ever after. Our families have accepted us and that speaks volumes about our love and how we're destined to hold each other close for the rest of our lives."

"You know what you've done for me," he said. "You've taught me how to love and I feel I owe that to you for the rest of my life." He pulled the chute and it fluttered to the ground.

"Awwww," she moaned. "That makes me so happy. I love you so much."

"I love you too."

The wind picked up outside. The naked branches of the elm tree tapped softly on the window. He stared at the ceiling, cradling her blond head in his right arm, pressing her firmly against his chest. She was breathing slowly, a mesmerizing rhythm that most nights put him to sleep. But tonight, unsure thoughts crept into his mind, swirling there like dead yellow leaves on the street outside.

Anxious aspirations. Familial expectations. Reluctant love. Racial obligations. It was as though she could hear these things. Or as though she could feel his intense gaze into the stuccoed ceiling bounce back at her.

She eventually fell asleep, but he lay there thinking for hours. His eyes wide open. His body tense as he held her tight. Not wanting to let her go, but not wanting to accept his self-enforced ideals about what his bloodline should be. The farther he went down this road with her, the greater his own doubt grew about what their future held and what he thought he wanted—all the while trying to deny the most virtuous love he had ever felt, a love that filled that room like an ever-expanding soft, sweet and virtuous fragrance spilling from the cracks in the windows and underneath the doors.

Rigid arms and sharp eyes ruptured the calm that had taken her so quickly to a peaceful sleep. She woke up knowing he hadn't been sleeping, and through the faint veil of darkness could see his dark eyes gazing upwards.

"What's wrong?" she asked.

He responded with such a hollow, distant "nothing" that she snapped awake right away. She had heard this "nothing" before and it was something she didn't like. This late at night, after all those emotions charged through their small bedroom and finally settled, and with discussions of their future from days past still fresh in both of their minds, she knew just what that "nothing" meant.

She took a deep breath and let out an obvious sigh. He knew what was coming, so he deliberately waited a few moments before following up with the obligatory "What?"

They lay a few seconds, eyes fixed on randomly chosen points in the dark. He was looking at the dome-shaped ceiling light. When it was on, he could see faint, molded curves in the frosted glass converging at the brass apex. It was an ugly glow. Like a lifeless, round, fake breast.

She looked outside through a crack in the blinds. The branch that tapped the window wavered back and forth with the wind, glowing an alien orange from the adjacent streetlight. The season left it naked, bare in the unwanted, ugly spotlight. It kept tapping away, like it wanted in. She usually took the window side of the bed for this very reason, even though she denied it at first.

"Are we seriously gonna talk about this again?" she asked.

"About what?" he replied, knowing full well.

"We can't help who we are or where we come

from. But I thought we loved each other? Isn't that enough?"

"Yeah … it is … "

"Well, what's the fucking problem?"

"Nothing."

Blank, frustrated stares into the ceiling ensued.

"It has been five years. Obviously it means something. I'm sick of you getting hung up on this bullshit."

"You don't know my family."

"You don't know MY family!"

"I bring a blond, white girl to the rez and everyone talks."

"Why do you care? I've been there a million times already!"

"I know. You'd never live there with me though."

"Yes I would!"

"Your parents would never want you to live there with me."

"Fuck my parents! I've been in this long enough to know this is real and I don't want anything else. Why isn't that enough for you?"

"We're not the same."

She sat up, blanketed the covers around her naked breasts and started to cry. "Fine. Fuck you."

He knew he had messed up but he didn't know how to fix it. It had been a perfect night. Everything was perfect with them. They did everything together. But he was still hung up on what he thought he was supposed to do. Something that trumped the most virtuous love he'd ever known.

The branches stopped tapping the window. The wind calmed to a slow murmur. And he was alone.

He poured two packets of brown sugar into his coffee, added ten per cent cream to lighten it up and stirred with a little wooden stick. This was the highlight of his day. He pulled his hat down tight and looked for a place out on the patio.

All these years later, he still loved these city streets. Watching everyone go by—students, young lovers, delivery dudes, suits. He opened the paper to read but couldn't concentrate, so he just watched people. Coming out of the subway backwards, he saw familiar blond hair. She was lugging something up the stairs, almost rolling it up, one step at a time. She turned around. It was her—pushing a beautiful little baby down the street. Blond hair, blue eyes—the most precious thing he'd ever seen. And they were coming his way.

He pulled his hat down tighter, folded the newspaper up under his arm, put his sunglasses on and left.

The circle was almost complete.

"*Chi-miigwetch*, my nieces and nephews. You've done very well. This was a very hot sweat, maybe too hot for your first time. But you made it this far and I'm proud of you. We have all told some very powerful stories tonight. What we've shared stays in here. This is only your beginning on the path to healing. You have told your Mother and she is here for you. She will always love you and care for you. We are here to try to guide you. That's what this place is for. It's our connection between our world and the Spirit World. This is where love and respect were born, just like in your mother's womb."

The Seven Grandfather rocks in the middle of the sweat lodge had cracked and some had split. Some were still a fading orange, illuminating the small space just ever so slightly. But they still kept the lodge hot. Small piles of tobacco and cedar ash nestled on top and in the cracks of the rocks. Hours had passed, but it seemed like minutes.

"We will hear from the last of you, then sing a travelling song."

There was a long, drawn out silence. They could hear the crackle of the fire outside. Everyone knew whose turn it was, and they waited for him to speak.

David Shkaabewis was uneasy through the whole ceremony. He tried to ignore everything he heard, and just bear the heat. He was only there because his wife asked him to go. The Elder was her uncle. He was on the brink of losing his job. He drank almost everyday. He hated hearing from his peers about how bad the past was and just wanted to move on. Moving on meant drinking as much as possible to forget everything.

He felt the invisible gaze of all the pairs of eyes on him. He let out a frustrated breath. "I'm not sayin' nothin' about any of this Indian bullshit. I don't even know why I'm here. I can't believe I sat through all this shit and listened to all of you cry. Fuckin' bullshit."

"You have to be respectful. We can't fight in the sweat lodge."

"Fuck you, old man. Let me outta here. NOW!"

"Open the flap."

The outside helper opened the canvas tarp to let him out. The piercing orange glow of the fire constricted pupils inside as the light shot in abruptly. A cool gust of outside air also eked into the sweatlodge. David got to his knees and quickly crawled out.

There was a brief awkward silence following David's offensive departure. But the Elder carried on, urging the others to keep the love and respect they shared in their hearts and spirits. "Our Mother and the Creator are forgiving," he said. "They will always guide our way, and keep the path clear for us, no matter how far we stray from it."

They said their last prayer and sang their last song. One by one they left, shivering once again, looking for their boots. Some left disappointed— their personal crises unresolved. They were worried their thoughts and prayers wouldn't make it to the Creator.

AASINAABE

Sometimes the sun forces the eyes open. And as much as the eyelids resist, it's hard to keep them shut. This is the harsh reality about waking up in a ditch. David knew it and tried to shake it off. But there was no getting around it. As soon as he stood up, he had to think about damage control. He wasn't sure where he was. There were birds chirping and it was hot. In the middle of summer the smell of the trees carried across the road. He wished he could lie back down in the ditch, but it wasn't that easy. This was home, unfortunately.

Shiny Beaches Island is on the eastern shore of Georgian Bay. It's home to the Ojibway reservation of Shiny Beaches (or "Indian Reserve No. 37"), under the treaty signed with the federal government in 1849. Its residents had now lived there for over a century and a half. They were forced upon the tiny portion of un-arable land by what would eventually become the Canadian government in order to settle a town there. For most of this period, life had been dismal. Just like life on any other reserve. Alcoholism, unemployment, disease, and suicide were rampant. The internal government was corrupt—a problem in many Native communities.

David was no stranger to that abuse. He liked to party too much and couldn't hold down a steady job. That's why looking in a mirror was beyond painful for him. Life on Shiny Beaches could not get any worse. But the island that held the nearly six hundred and fifty people was unique—the people there just didn't know how, nor were they ready to understand. Despite all that, David was at the brink. No one knew what he knew, and what he didn't want to know.

❊

Another wasted night and David Shkaabewis crossed the bridge from the mainland to the island, staggering in a drunken stupor. The 25-year-old was returning from the nearby town of Davis Mills where he was kicked out of the Roadhouse Bar for fighting. It was 3:00 a.m. and he had already been walking for half an hour. Home was another hour away and David had to be up by 7:00 a.m. to be at the pulp mill for work.

He looked up and saw the sky getting light at the horizon. The soft, early morning summer wind blew in a sweet caress and he knew this was the last fulfilling moment he would have that day. Sometimes walking back through the rez was sobering.

And then he was home.

Crashing through his front door like a battering ram, David fell to the floor in a heap and passed out. The crash was like a vicious bull on parade.

David's wife, Sharon, rolled over in her bed. "Shit, not again," she said to herself. Frightened and concerned—but irritated—she got up and went to see how bad his condition was. On her way she saw Evan standing at his bedroom door. Sleepy-eyed, but concerned, he was still trying to figure out what he thought of his dad.

With beautiful naiveté, he said, "Mommy, what happened?"

"Go back to bed," she said, annoyed and uneasy. Sharon didn't want to subject her five-year-old son to any more of his father's alcoholism. Evan sheepishly returned to the quiet sanctuary of his small room.

Making her way to the entrance of the one-storey, two-bedroom house, Sharon could feel the cooling summer gust blowing through the wide-open front door. She saw her husband and her son's role model face down on the floor, unconscious. This was the man she fell in love with when they were in Grade Two. The small boy she had a crush on in that one-room schoolhouse.

"Dave!" she said. Nothing. She may as well have been talking to a corpse. She kicked him swiftly in the side but all it did was make him snore. Sharon was a small woman, no match for David's two-hundred-pound frame. There was no way she could carry him to bed. She really didn't feel like sleeping beside filth anyway. So David was left on the floor for the rest of the morning.

Three hours later, Sharon tried to get him back up for work. "Dave, you're late!" she shouted. "Wake up, for Christ's sake!" She picked up a bucket full of water left on the floor to catch raindrops through the leaky roof the night before. She doused his pale face and he was finally roused. In a daze, David shot up. Eyes bloodshot. "Where the fuck am I?" he thought. "What happened?" He looked up to see his wife standing over him. Evan sat at the table, eating a bowl of cereal, an innocent child looking for some kind of calm at the bottom of a bowl. Hoping and wishing the people he loved the most wouldn't yell.

David's head pounded. Last night came back like a flood.

"Fuck you!" he yelled.

Uncontrollable impulses are characteristic of an alcoholic. Something was about to happen, so Evan abandoned his half-eaten bowl of cereal and retreated to his room, plugging his ears along the way. David struggled to his feet. His head continued to pound and the room began to spin. He glared at Sharon angrily. Her eyes shot back with intense resentment.

"What kind of father are you?" she screamed. "Your son is scared shitless of you!"

"Don't tell me how to be a fuckin' father!" He threw a punch that was meant to hurt. It caught her right on the left cheekbone, making a sharp crack.

Sharon crumpled to the floor. She didn't want to move nor make a noise because she knew he would hit her again, but the pain was immense. She felt her face throb and her soul cry. Tears of pain and sorrow soaked her eyes and rolled to the floor. How could someone who said he loved you make you hurt so bad? When Monday morning came around, there'd be a black eye to explain. "I left one of the cupboard doors open when I was baking," she'd say. "I turned back from the stove to get some more oil and didn't notice. My cheek ran right into it." She hadn't used one like that in a while, so she hoped it would fly.

She looked up and saw him sweep in for another strike. She rolled over quickly and shrank into a turtle position as best as she could, awaiting another hit in the back of the head or the kidneys. It didn't come. Still bracing, she turned her head slightly to see David almost paralyzed in shame. Evan had returned from his room in the middle of the assault, and watched his father readying to hit his mother again. He caught David's eye, and that's what made the attack stop.

Evan stared at his dad's clenched fists. David noticed, and looked down at his throbbing right hand. Evan's scared and confused glare pried David's hands open. He looked down and they were trembling. David looked back at Sharon, crying and crumpled on the floor, with a bright pink welt on her left cheek. She sobbed harder when she realized her son saw some of this. Afraid, the father held back an outburst of tears and stormed out the door. Having lost all valour, the soldier retreated. The boy ran to his mother, and buried his face in her neck as she trembled on the floor. They both wept.

Chief Susan Wawashkesh arrived early at the band office. She had told her husband, Hubert, that she had to catch up on some work. It required explanation because nobody goes to work at the band office early. The sun was already blazing in the morning sky and shone through the window of her corner office. The blinds fragmented the light into parallel yellow lines, refracted on the opposite wall. They highlighted one particular medicine wheel—a symbol of balance and harmony—that hung on the wall adjacent to her desk. Ignoring the natural beauty, she drew the blinds shut. She booted up her computer and sat down, waiting for it to start. The hums and whirs seemed heavy today. She knew what she was doing. A few double clicks and something opened up called "Fall Travel Expenses"—an outline in the annual budget showing what she thought she would need for travel for the rest of the year. The elected representative of the Shiny Beaches people—the person they trusted—drew up a cheque for $10,000 and typed in the letter that she was extracting $4,000 from the band's account for her "extensive traveling needs."

She did it all without skipping a beat or thinking twice.

The unknown soldier didn't try to find a ride into town for work. Already late and still feeling the foggy and lingering effects of alcohol, David knew he would no longer have a job. The light seemed clearer and the sounds seemed louder. The bright sun above the birch and songbirds pierced his tainted ears. Songs that should have reminded him of something fell to the ground and shattered like a premature autumn. So he wandered, aimlessly.

He was on the eastern side of the island, not far from his childhood home. Elevating shimmerings of his youth, he entered the thick forest and made his way to the fox-run his father took him to as a child. His father died of an alcohol-related hunting mishap when David was only eight years old. Some people on the reserve mentioned "suicide" and Alfred Shkaabewis in the same sentence, but never in front of his kids. David's mother, Priscilla, was left to take care of him, his two brothers and four sisters on her own. It was a tough childhood with no father for most of it, and he never learned to be one.

David made his way through the tall maple and oak trees. He was almost at the clearing where the fox-run was, but the thicket held him back. The thorns the blackberry bushes held were like barbed wire—digging and stinging his now bare arms with each step. He could see the trail from where he stood. Determined—his heart longing for a simpler and happier time—he tore his way through, arms bleeding. He made it to the other side of the brush and looked around. His oasis of sentiment hadn't changed much in twenty years. Some trees were taller but that was about it. He sat on the ground and lit a cigarette, waiting for tiny cat-like foxes to dart across the trail. The sun was high, gleaming onto his long, sunken face. He felt like a war veteran, returning to a battleground where he once fought, astonished to realize the emptiness of the place. But the spirits and ghosts pulled the air down and his heart with it.

Half an hour passed and there were no foxes. Sadness came once again.

Confusion followed frustration. He got up, brushed himself off and decided to walk down the worn trail. It was something he had never done, or even contemplated. As a child he was afraid of how the path meandered seemingly into oblivion, but now he was interested.

As he entered these new surroundings, a grim darkness enveloped him. Tall trees obscured the sky above him. Rustling leaves and branches silently hustled him, broken by the occasional crack of a twig. The melodious songs of various birds, reassuring him of his safety added to the cacophony.

He saw another clearing ahead, sunlight penetrating the canopy. As he walked towards it, the light became stronger. "What was on the other side?" he wondered. "Why do I come here?" His head was swimming.

He stepped out of the forest. Everything seemed to miraculously open up like a natural revelation, and it was the most beautiful sight he had ever experienced. He was standing on a cliff, twenty meters high, overlooking a small inlet that opened to the great Georgian Bay. Dark evergreens lined the hills and cliffs along the shore. The water itself was so calm; it was like a mirror reflecting a raw natural beauty to whoever looked from above. To his right, a few hundred yards away, was a long beach of golden sand. David couldn't look away. He smiled and wanted to go swimming. The water was so pure and clean that he could almost see life's cycles functioning through the nourishing liquid. Huge white stones lined the rim of the cove and the trees were tall and green. The shining sun enhanced the purity of the place. Ecstasy overcame him. His eyes wandered back to the beach of gold. He wanted to go there.

The cliff gradually receded as he made his way to the beach. David could already picture himself lying on that blond mattress, reaping nature's sheer beauty. Suddenly, the picture before him shook and dropped as he lost his footing. He looked down to see that he had stepped into a crevice.

"AHH FUCK!" It was the first noise that came from his mouth in many hours. His ankle was twisted and the rough rocks scraped his shin. It wasn't bleeding too badly, though. He pulled his leg out, dusted himself off, and looked down between the massive rocks. The crack ran all the way to the bottom, the walls running perfectly parallel. It was as if the Creator had lifted a totally symmetrical monolith out of the cliff—at the bottom, no rock whatsoever. But this wasn't the spectacle that blew his mind. Something else caught his eye below. About three metres down from where he was standing was a rock, lodged in the crevice—a perfect, smooth, ivory sphere. The sun was now at its apex, shining a peculiar spotlight on the orb. It glistened brightly off one half of the stone, nearly blinding him, but it cast a shadow as well, rendering the adjacent half of the stone as dark as night.

David had to have this rock. It infatuated him. He couldn't reach it from above, so he climbed precariously down and stretched his arm from the face of the cliff. He stood on a thin ledge, grasping a branch that jutted out for balance. Securing his hold, he reached into the crack, straining to clutch the enigmatic white orb. He was standing in the vast shadow of the cliff, invisible in the mighty shade of Mother Earth. David reached further and further. His lips pressed tightly together as beads of sweat lined his forehead and marched down his face. His fingers were within inches of the stone. Closer ... and closer ... suddenly the entire cliff began to tremor.

David looked up as dark, seemingly diseased clouds rushed overhead, blocking out the sun. The leaves on the trees instantly faded and crumbled. It was like ash from a bonfire falling to the ground. The luscious, brown bark of the trees turned a splintering grey while they decomposed in their ancient stance.

The wind picked up in a violent maelstrom and the water raged beneath in a turbulent grey pool. He looked back to the beach and the once enthralling view now portrayed a ghastly image of death. The yellow sand was now black, as though singed by some supernatural authority. Dull monolithic stones erupted from beneath, violently piercing the beach.

Frightened, David pulled his arm from the gap. The wind stopped and the water turned still, but everything remained deathly. "This is the Spirit World," David thought. "I'm dead." He brought himself to his feet at the top of the precipice. He turned to look at his paradise lost. Each tree remained grey and bare. The huge stones still stood erect on the beach. David felt an unsettling insecurity, but not simply about his own mortality—this was something bigger.

He turned and ran back down the trail.

⁂

Hank Rawlings was the reserve's police officer. Non-Native himself, he was appointed by Chief Wawashkesh at the beginning of her term. As a child, Hank dreamed of being a cop and serving the good of society. Those dreams and ideals slowly faded once greed and opportunity overcame him.

On this particular rainy afternoon, Hank was on his way to Bill Eagle's house, one of the reserve's elected councillors. Officer Rawlings was making a delivery. He drove his black Ford Explorer slowly up the driveway in order to avoid the downpour. He grabbed an attaché case sitting in the passenger seat, got out, and sprinted up to the front door and knocked. As he waited, he held the case over his salt-and-pepper hair for shelter. Bill opened the door, and before saying anything, invited Hank in with a smile. Hank took off his boots and followed Bill to the kitchen table, just steps from the front door.

"I have an interesting proposal for you," said the cop.

"If it's what I think it is, a certain member of the local police force will get a raise," said the councillor.

"Big bust at the high school today.

"How much?"

"This much," Hank pulled a quarter pound of marijuana and an eight-ball of cocaine out of the case.

"Right on."

"You got what you want. So we don't have to dance at the pow wow, if you know what I mean."

"Don't worry. We've found a few creative ways of sneaking five G's past INAC. But I'll be expecting monthly deliveries as long as you've got access."

"That's a treaty." Grinning, Hank peered down at his watch. "I should be going."

"Sure you don't wanna stick around for a blast?"

"Well," the officer sarcastically replied, "if you're gonna fire up the peace pipe, then sure."

Bill got up and walked over to the drawer left of the kitchen sink. He opened it and pulled out a foggy mirror and a razor blade.

Five days had passed since David's jolting experience with the mysterious white orb. He was confused. He hadn't had a drop of booze since and remained morose. Sharon prodded him, asking what was wrong.

"Nothing," he replied. "Don't worry about it."

David didn't know what to do and slowly isolated himself from the people around him. He figured what happened at the inlet had a deep and significant spiritual meaning. It swam through his slowly clearing mind for hours at a time, but he was reluctant to tell anyone about it. He wished he had listened and cared more at that sweatlodge with Sharon's uncle back in the winter. On this partly cloudy and chilly June afternoon he felt afraid and ashamed. He decided he had to tell someone, someone still in touch with the old ways. Someone firmly grounded and stable. David had to understand.

He called up his old drinking buddy, Jim Two Rivers. As teens they would frequently scrape up money for a case of beer and find any old clearing in the bush to drink. They didn't know why they felt compelled to drink. They just did. It was their regular weekend mission which expanded to weekdays as they got older and dropped out of high school. Sometimes there were parties, sometimes others— cousins, friends—tagged along, and sometimes it was just the two of them. They were escaping something, but they never talked about it. They didn't have to. Subconsciously they were aware of each other's plight as lost, bitter, confused Anishinaabe youth. They had a lot of the same problems, but they were both individuals with unique ambitions beyond the reserve. They talked about a lot of things back then—dreams of careers and riches that would never be realized, plans to turn around the community and make it the happy and proud place the Elders claimed it once was. They even planned to learn Ojibway properly. They both swore to kick the bottle. Ten years later, Jim had. David still had a ways to go.

The phone rang. "*Aanii*," answered Jim.

"*Aanii* Jim," David answered with nervous urgency and forced enthusiasm in his voice. "It's, uh, Dave."

Apart from seeing each other briefly at the band office a few times, it had been a while since they had any kind of conversation. "How you doin'?" asked Jim.

"Ah, alright. Not working right now. But it's alright. You?"

"Pretty good! How's the family?"

"They're good. Evan's five now!"

And before long, David leaped into the story, bluntly and without bombast. His voice trembled as it picked up momentum. He had never spoken so emotionally to his childhood friend, even after seventeen bottles of beer. David eloquently told of the collective beauty of the place, being specific about the rock and the beach. He even surprised himself the way he was able to describe it. Even retelling it made the hair at the back of his neck stand as a cold shiver ran through his body. He explained how the beauty vanished after he tried to grasp the white orb. Tears rolled down his face like raindrops beading down a cold, dry stone.

He finished his story. There was a long, cold pause on Jim's end. David cleared his throat, reached for a cigarette and lit it.

"How did you feel, Dave, when you saw that change?" Jim finally asked. "What did you see?"

"I … it was … the end," replied David.

"The end of what?"

"The end of everything! I saw and felt death, Jimbo. The fuckin' end. But not just mine. We all died there!" He struggled to prevent himself from sobbing and it made his whole entire body heave.

On the other end of the line, Jim was silent. Without consolation, he said, "I'm coming over and you're gonna take me to this place."

Within minutes, Jim ripped up David's driveway

in his pickup truck. David was sitting on his front step. He butted out the smoke he lit halfway through their brief chat and jumped in the truck. Jim quickly backed up to turn out of the driveway, kicking up a thin cloud of beige dust.

"You okay?" Jim asked.

David's hands were still shaking. "Yeah, I'm cool," he said.

The rest of the drive was quiet. David fixed his gaze on the passing ferns in the ditch. Jim gripped the wheel with both hands, staring at the road, wondering what he was about to see.

They made it to the clearing where David had sat days earlier—where his childhood went up in vaporous trails of bitterness and pain. They got out and David led the way. Encompassed in fear, he began to run. Jim struggled to keep up. It grew dark as they neared the place. At this point, Jim got scared. He knew the stories about the rock David had described. Now it was becoming present—and real. David, meanwhile, still didn't understand, but he knew it was bigger than life. A gloomy realization crept up both of their backs, but there was no way they would tell each other. Jim was now running faster, ahead of David. It felt as if they were running to the gallows, the guillotine, the firing line, or that final path the Great Spirit sends you along before you enter the eternal mystery of the Spirit World.

Jim reached the cliff ahead of David. The immense grey sepulchres were now gone, but the sand was ashen. The water was calm but dull, as if bad spirits festered in its murky abyss. The trees arms sagged, as if brought to the threshold of death, but cruelly allowed to suffer for a few moments longer. Dark clouds lined the sky.

As soon as David caught up, Jim grabbed him by the collar—a crazed look in his eyes—and shouted, "Show me, now!"

David led Jim to the crevice and pointed down at the round rock. "There," he murmured. Jim lowered his brown eyes to the icon and his jaw dropped.

There they stood, frozen in fear and wonder. David looked at his childhood friend, slightly hunched over, mouth agape, staring down a perfectly parallel crevice in a cliff. It looked as if he was struggling to say something.

"What is it?" whispered David.

Jim dropped to his knees on the rough grey rock beneath him, gasping for breath. "Nothing can prepare you for the truth but you have to know," he struggled to say.

Jim pulled his legs from underneath him to sit on his behind. He crossed his legs and dropped his heavy onto his bent knees. David slowly crouched down to his left, and sat just like him, staring at the profile of his old friend. Jim took a deep breath, heaving as he exhaled.

"There was a time, believe it or not, when we had lost our way even worse than we have now. Even before the arrival of the white man. Our people began to abandon the old ways, living life in an unwholesome and unbalanced way. As Anishinaabe people, we fought in long wars against the people of the plains to fulfill our own greed. This was long before we had the drum.

"The Creator threatened to wipe us out in order to cleanse Mother Earth. There was a great flood, and only a few of us lived to start over. We did, under the premise of living a pure and wholesome way once more. But today, we've lost our way much like before. Our chief is selling us out, taking the fuckin' money, keeping the kids high. But back then the great eagle spoke for us and that's why we're so grateful to the eagle today."

He stared down at the orb again, which had grown

dark. "A condition was set: that a rock, perfectly round, would be placed in a location where no one could interfere with it. No one was supposed to touch it. This stone emulated the body of our beautiful Mother—of Mother Earth. One day, this rock—called "*Aasinaabe*" by the Creator—will fall into the water below. This contact between Mother Earth's body and her blood will trigger another cleansing. If all of humankind has been generally balanced, then the Creator will replenish the earth, making everything pure again and leaving us natural, in unity with Mother Earth, to live eternally in peace and harmony.

"But if the Creator sees us as unbalanced after this rock has fallen, our lives will end. What you see before you, David, is *Aasinaabe*, or the stone of cleansing."

David felt paralyzed. He couldn't move or speak. As this revelation sank in, he feared for his wife and son.

Weeks later David was sitting at the kitchen table with Evan. "Drink the rest of the milk in that bowl," he told his son. "You need that to make your bones strong." It was an enjoyably clear and sober Saturday morning for David. "Hurry up, or we won't play catch!"

"But I don't like milk, Daddy!" replied Evan.

"If you don't like it, why do you put it on your cereal?"

"Oh yeah, I guess I do then." He giggled, and David smiled.

"Go get your glove."

Evan ran to his room. He'd be six in the fall. Almost time to start learning about sports. David smiled as his eyes followed his son down the hall.

Sharon was standing at the counter, finishing up the dishes. She turned around to face David, still sitting at the table. "You know," she said, "You've done pretty good lately. When's the last time you drank?"

"I dunno," he said. "A while ago."

"Why?"

"I'll tell you someday soon. But I can tell you right now—I'm gonna try my hardest not to drink again."

Sharon smiled hopefully. She was doubtful, but had faith in her husband and the family they had created. She wanted to believe him.

Months later, and David stuck to his word. He quit drinking and devoted more time to his wife and child. He wondered what she would be making for supper as he walked through the halls of Davis Mills High School, returning to class after lunch. He had

gone back to high school for a semester to finally
obtain his diploma so he could move on to college
and finally work towards living in those good ways
he dreamed of as a child.

But the cycles of abuse and corruption continued on
Shiny Beaches. The people ignored the old ways.
Drug and alcohol abuse was higher than ever and
men continued to beat their wives and children. The
governing body—those elected by the people—
continued to embezzle money and abuse its power.
Life was still dismal for many, but David and Jim
took it upon themselves to try to keep the old ways
alive. They started a drum group with some of the
young men. They held youth sweats late at night on
the weekend. David was brushing up on his Ojibway
and teaching Evan.

Then one June afternoon, at 2:15 p.m., an earthquake
shook central Ontario for nearly a minute. The last
time that happened in these parts was five decades

ago. The Elders remembered it well. It measured 5.9 on the Richter scale. Trees fell in the forest. Dogs stopped dead in their tracks. People screamed and ran for their lives. Fires and explosions ignited everywhere. The tremor opened the crevice half a centimetre wider.

Aasinaabe fell. When it hit the water it split into four equal parts—one red, one yellow, one white, and one black—and sank.

David, Sharon and Evan were all home. The quake broke windows and knocked dishes out of the open cupboards. "You guys okay?" David asked as he ran inside. He hugged them both, squeezing hard with nervous tension in his arms. He expected Jim to rip up his gravel driveway again. Within minutes he did.

They didn't speak. Jim drove his pickup with white knuckles on the steering wheel all the way to the clearing. He slammed on the brakes and they threw open the doors. Jim grabbed his tobacco pouch and jumped out. The truck doors remained open.

They ran along the same trail they charged through a year ago. Branches scraped their faces and bare arms, but they didn't notice. They approached the cliff where some of the scorched trees were once again showing signs of life. Tiny twigs with leaves jutted out from the blistered bark.

Their feet pounded all the way to the edge of the cliff. Jim slipped slightly and David grabbed him just before he rolled off into the water below. They shared a quick, scared glance and dropped to their hands and knees on either side of the crevice. They looked down and saw that the orb was gone. They slowly looked up at each other. Their eyes met, and they held their breath, waiting.